Dear Parents:

Congratulations! Your child is taking the first steps on an exciting journey. The destination? Independent reading!

STEP INTO READING® will help your child get there. The program offers five steps to reading success. Each step includes fun stories and colorful art or photographs. In addition to original fiction and books with favorite characters, there are Step into Reading Non-Fiction Readers, Phonics Readers and Boxed Sets, Sticker Readers, and Comic Readers—a complete literacy program with something to interest every child.

Learning to Read, Step by Step!

Ready to Read   Preschool–Kindergarten
• big type and easy words • rhyme and rhythm • picture clues
For children who know the alphabet and are eager to begin reading.

Reading with Help   Preschool–Grade 1
• basic vocabulary • short sentences • simple stories
For children who recognize familiar words and sound out new words with help.

Reading on Your Own   Grades 1–3
• engaging characters • easy-to-follow plots • popular topics
For children who are ready to read on their own.

Reading Paragraphs   Grades 2–3
• challenging vocabulary • short paragraphs • exciting stories
For newly independent readers who read simple sentences with confidence.

Ready for Chapters   Grades 2–4
• chapters • longer paragraphs • full-color art
For children who want to take the plunge into chapter books but still like colorful pictures.

STEP INTO READING® is designed to give every child a successful reading experience. The grade levels are only guides; children will progress through the steps at their own speed, developing confidence in their reading. The F&P Text Level on the back cover serves as another tool to help you choose the right book for your child.

Remember, a lifetime love of reading starts with a single step!

To brave fire fighters
everywhere! Thank you
for looking after all of us!

Step into Reading, Random House, and the Random House colophon are registered trademarks of Penguin Random House LLC.

Visit us on the Web!
StepIntoReading.com
randomhousekids.com
RichardScarryBooks.com

Educators and librarians, for a variety of teaching tools, visit us at
RHTeachersLibrarians.com

Library of Congress Cataloging-in-Publication Data
Scarry, Richard.
Richard Scarry's Smokey the fireman.
   pages cm. — (Step into reading)
"Originally published in a slightly different form by Golden Books, New York, in 1988."
—Copyright page.
Summary: The adventures of a fire fighter at work and on his day off.
ISBN 978-0-385-39140-5 (pbk.) — ISBN 978-0-375-97363-5 (lib. bdg.) —
ISBN 978-0-385-39141-2 (ebook)
[1. Fire fighters—Fiction. 2. Animals—Fiction.] I. Title. II. Title: Smokey the fireman.
PZ7.S327Roc 2015 [E]—dc23 2014002176

Printed in the United States of America
10 9 8 7 6 5 4 3 2

This book has been officially leveled by using the F&P Text Level Gradient™ Leveling System.

Richard Scarry's
SMOKEY THE FIREMAN

Random House 🏠 New York

Smokey was a fire fighter.

He loved to put out fires.

One day

Smokey was asleep

in the firehouse.

Down the street
there was a fire!
"Help!" cried Katie Kitty.
"My house is full of smoke!"

Clang, clang, went the bell.

Smokey jumped up.

He put on his hat,

his boots,

and his raincoat.

He slid down the pole
right into his fire engine!

Smokey drove fast.

Officer Bob stopped

the cars.

Hurry, Smokey!

Oh, no!

A pie truck!

CRASH!

Pies went flying.

The pieman went flying, too.

They all landed in
Smokey's fire engine!

Smokey kept going.

Katie Kitty needed help.

Smokey rescued Katie Kitty.

"Thank you, Smokey!" she said.

Then Smokey turned his hose
on the fire.

SWOOOSH!

The fire was out.

Smokey turned his hose

on his fire engine.

SWOOOSH!

His fire engine was

red again.

Smokey turned his hose
on the pieman.
SWOOOSH!
The pieman was
clean again.

Everyone went inside
to see what the fire
was all about.

Oh, my! A pie had burned.

Lucky for them,

Katie had another pie.

They ate it all up!

The next day

was Smokey's day off

from work.

He invited Katie for

a day in the country.

So Smokey and Katie
went on a picnic.
They brought sandwiches
and milk for lunch.
And four blueberry pies!

They watched frogs swimming.

It was very quiet.

Smokey almost fell asleep.

All at once

they heard shouting.

"Help! Help! Come quick!"

"Our barn is on fire!"

shouted Pat and Penny Pig.

"We will help!" said Smokey.

Smokey had to think fast.

He did not have his fire engine.

"Quick!" shouted Smokey.

"We must go to the well!"

There they met Farmer Fox.

He wanted to help, too.

Smokey told them
what to do.

Pat drew water from the well.
Penny and Katie gave
buckets of water to Smokey.

Smokey was up on a ladder.

Smokey threw water
on the fire.
Then he threw down
the empty buckets.

Farmer Fox gave the buckets

to Pat to refill.

Pat filled them over and over.

Soon the fire was out.

"Thank you, Smokey!"
said Pat and Penny.
"You saved our barn."

"Now we can rest,"
said Smokey.
And they all ate lots of pie!